My X Y Z Book

by Jane Belk Moncure
illustrated by Linda Hohag

THE CHILD'S WORLD

ELGIN, ILLINOIS 60120

Library of Congress Cataloging in Publication Data

Moncure, Jane Belk.
  My "xyz" book.

  (My first steps to reading)
  Rev. ed. of: My x, y, z sound box. © 1979.
  Summary: Little x, Little y, and Little z fill
their boxes with things that begin with the letters
x, y, and z.
    1. Children's stories, American.   [1. Alphabet]
I. Hohag, Linda. ill.   II. Moncure, Jane Belk.   My
x, y, z, sound box.   III. Title.   IV. Series: Moncure,
Jane Belk.   My first steps to reading.
PZ7.M739Myx   1984   [E]   84-17561
ISBN 0-89565-295-1

Distributed by Childrens Press, 1224 West Van Buren Street,
Chicago, Illinois 60607.

My "x, y, z" Book

Little  had a box.

He said, "I will fill my 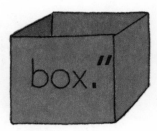 box."

Little found an

x-ray machine.

"Excellent," said Little  .

"With my x-ray
                machine,

I can see inside of things."

He made
an x-ray of
his hands.

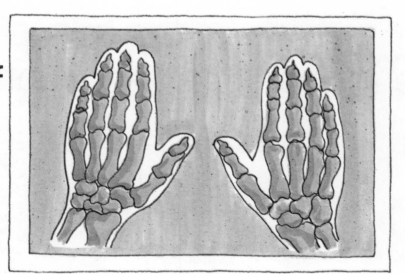

He could see his bones.
"Excellent," he said.

He put the x-ray picture
into his 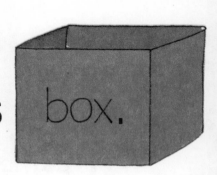 box.

He made an x-ray of his feet.

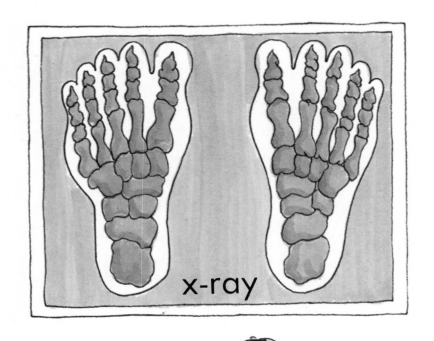

x-ray

"Excellent," Little said. "I can see the bones in my feet."

Then he put the
x-ray picture
and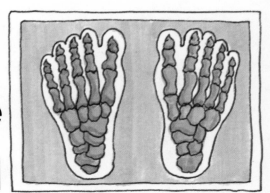
the x-ray machine

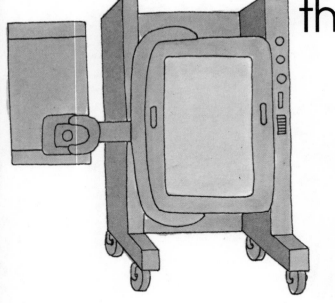

into his  box.

He said, "Now I will
call my friend…

Little . He may have a box."

"I do," said Little .

"I will fill my box too."

Little   found a   yo-yo.

It was a yellow yo-yo.

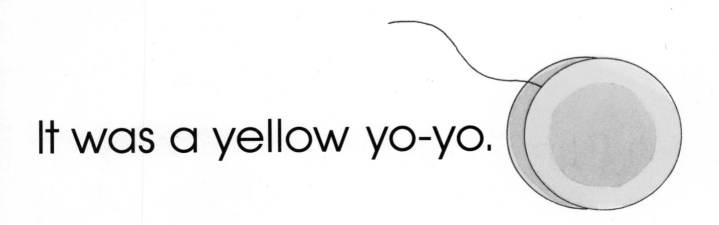

He tried to make the
yo-yo go up

and
down.

But the string was too short.

Little  found yarn.

He tied the yarn
to the yo-yo string.

Now the yo-yo went

down

and up,

down

and up.

Little  turned the box upside down.

He stood on the box.
His yo-yo went way down, and way up.
He said, "I will call my friend…

Little  and see if she

has a  box."

"I do," said Little .

"I will fill my box, too."

She found a zebra...

and two
more zebras.

Little  found three zebras,

one,

two,

three.

box

"In you go," she said.

box

But the zebras jumped
out of the box, zip, zip.

Away they ran,
zig-zag

down the   road.

Guess who ran after them?

Guess where they went?

They went to
the zoo.

More about Little X.

Sometimes "x" sounds like "z."
as in these words. Read them.

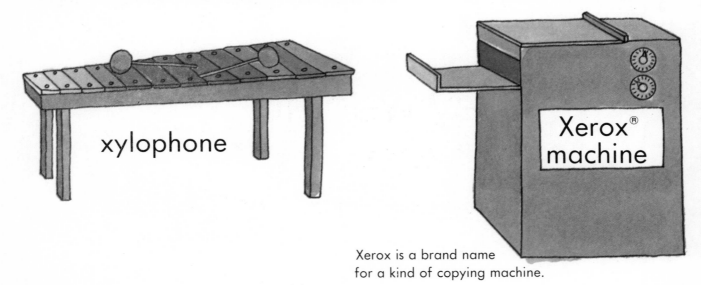

xylophone

Xerox® machine

Xerox is a brand name
for a kind of copying machine.

More words with Little .

yams

yacht

yard

yak

29

More words with Little .

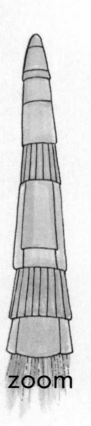
zoom

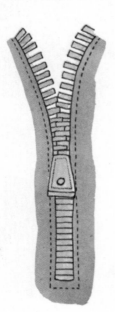
zipper

zinnia

zero
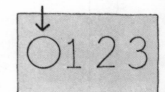

30